The Star Bright Factory

Nancy Libbey Mills
Illustrations by Holly Lynette Hagan

Special thanks to Mike Daniels
and specialer thanks to my darling Molly

Send written requests to:
PieintheSkyPublishing@msn.com

303-773-0851

www.PieintheSkyPublishing.com

Library of Congress Control Number
2015948057

ISBN
978-1-893815-23-0
First Edition
Printed in the USA

Pie in the Sky
PUBLISHING

For Jack and Caroline.
the shining stars in my life.

Jet Adore!

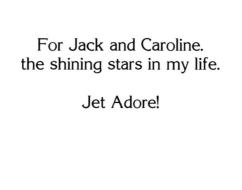

For Jeanne McCulloch,
my high school art teacher

HLH

Good night, sleep tight, we'll tiptoe out,

you had a drink, we read a book,

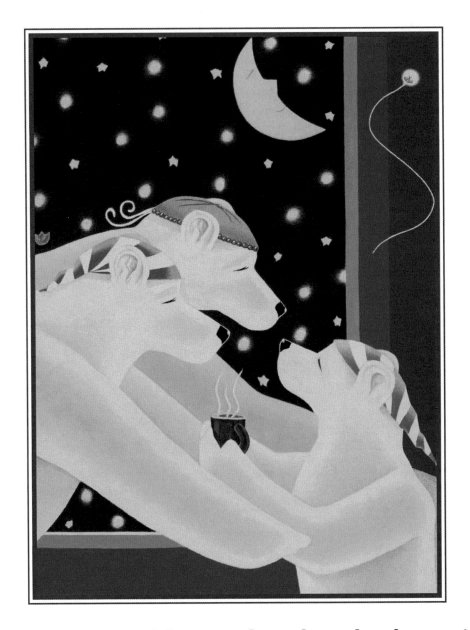

we kissed and hugged and tucked you in,

and made wishes on bright stars.

You close your eyes and drift to sleep and
while you dream, do you ever think,

what happens while you're not awake
outside up in the sky?

All those stars and galaxies, the man and moon,
are they the same;

how many moons I couldn't count,
and is every moon a man?

The secret's here but you can't tell,

where the stars come from
and why they fall,

from a place so high that you can't see,

it's called The Star Bright Factory.

They make the stars with extra care,
they make the stars those special bears,

they launch the stars so high and bright,
so all those stars can light the night.

The dippers are the catapults; they fill them full
with stars, stardust,

they pull it back and let them fly,
"The Milky Way or Bust!"

Mondays they make moonbeams,

Tuesdays are for twinkles,

Wednesday's wondrous,

Thursday's thunderous,
the skies are brightly sprinkled;

Friday's stars are falling,

Saturday's sparkle bright,

Sunday's are for swinging,
moonbeam jar lids fit on tight.

Why don't they fall you wonder?

Well, Friday's are made that way,

the rest are dipped in glue then launched,
shooting stars are on their way;

so every night you slumber, new stars
stick up with glue,

so when you wish you may you might,
your wishes can come true.

From the beach house where the sun always shines

...and the tulips are always in bloom.

Made in the USA
Middletown, DE
09 February 2021